big NATE

WELCOME TO MY WORLD

More

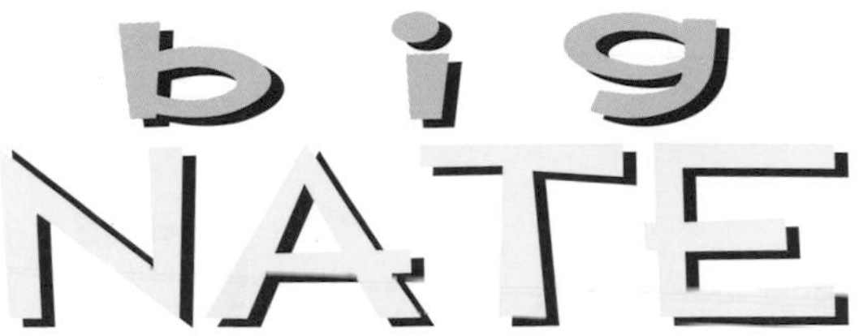

adventures from

LINCOLN PEIRCE

Big Nate From the Top

Big Nate Out Loud

Big Nate and Friends

Big Nate Makes the Grade

Big Nate All Work and No Play

Big Nate: Game On!

Big Nate: I Can't Take It!

Big Nate: Great Minds Think Alike

Big Nate: The Crowd Goes Wild!

Big Nate's Greatest Hits

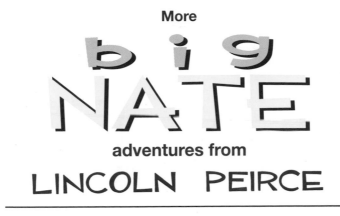

Big Nate: Say Good-bye to Dork City

big NATE

WELCOME TO MY WORLD

by LINCOLN PEIRCE

Kansas City • Sydney • London

WMPG

NATE, CAN YOU... UM... FIND OUT IF HEATHER LIKES ME?
LEAVE IT TO ME!

HEY, HEATHER, CAN I ASK YOU SOME-THING?
SURE!

DO YOU LIKE CHAD?
DEFINITELY!

YOU DO?
WHAT'S NOT TO LIKE? HE'S SO NICE! I MEAN, WHAT A SWEETIE!

HE'S SMART, HE'S FUNNY... HE'S GREAT! OF COURSE I LIKE CHAD! I LOVE CHAD!

...AS A FRIEND.

I'VE GOT GOOD NEWS AND BAD NEWS.
Peirce

LOOK WHO'S HERE!
HI GRAM! HI GRAMPS!

NATE, WE'RE REALLY LOOKING FORWARD TO GRANDPARENTS DAY AT YOUR SCHOOL!
YEAH, BUT **WHY?**
Peirce

I MEAN, WHEN **I'M** EIGHTY, I'M NOT GOING TO WANT TO HANG OUT AT A MIDDLE SCHOOL!

SON, FROM WHAT I HEAR, WHEN YOU'RE EIGHTY, YOU MIGHT STILL BE **IN** MIDDLE SCHOOL!
OH, VERN! HONESTLY!

THERE'S MY SCHOOL: P.S. 38.

LOOKS LIKE A SCHOOL, ALL RIGHT!
I THINK IT LOOKS **WONDERFUL!**

I CAN'T WAIT TO SEE YOUR CLASSROOMS AND MEET ALL YOUR TEACHERS! THIS IS SO **EXCITING!**

IT IS?
WE DON'T GET OUT MUCH.
QUIET, VERN.
Peirce

WHAT WILL YOU SHOW US FIRST, NATE?
WELL, THIS IS THE FRONT HALL... AND THAT'S THE DISPLAY CASE.
WELCO to GRANDPA DAY

IT'S MOSTLY FILLED WITH ACADEMIC TROPHIES AND STUFF...
OOH! ARE ANY OF THEM **YOUR** TROPHIES?

HA HA HA HA HA HA HA HA HA HA

WELL, **THAT'S** RUDE!
HEY! **PACK** IT, SCRUBS!
peirce

BEFORE HOMEROOM, I HAVE TO STOP BY MY LOCKER.
FAIR ENOUGH!

ALL THE SIXTH GRADE LOCKERS ARE ALONG THIS WALL.
OOH! WHICH ONE'S YOURS?

NEVER MIND.
STAND BACK.
Peirce

WE DIDN'T EVEN HAVE LOCKERS WHEN I WAS...
RRRINNG!
OH NO!

WHAT'S WRONG, NATE?
THE BELL! WE'RE LATE FOR HOME-ROOM! COME ON!

WELL, GOODNESS, WON'T IT BE OKAY TO BE LATE BY A FEW SECONDS?
NOT IN MRS. GODFREY'S CLASS! RUN!

WON'T GRANDPARENTS DAY LOSE SOME OF ITS LUSTER IF ONE OF THE GRANDPARENTS HAS A HEART ATTACK?
GASP!
I'M HERE! I MADE IT!
Peirce

YOU'RE TWENTY SECONDS LATE. THAT MEANS DETENTION.
WAIT! I MEAN, YES, I WAS LATE, BUT...

I WAS SHOWING MY GRAND-PARENTS AROUND, AND...
THAT'S HARDLY AN EXCUSE.

YOUR CLASSMATES ARE ALL HOSTING **THEIR** GRANDPARENTS, AND **THEY** SOMEHOW MADE IT TO CLASS ON TIME.
THE GREAT
Peirce

WHAT A...
QUIET, VERN.
WELCOME TO MY WORLD.

QUIZ TIME, PEOPLE. PUT AWAY YOUR NOTEBOOKS AND...
WHAT? HOLD IT!

IS THERE A PROBLEM, NATE?
YES, THERE'S A PROBLEM! YOU'RE GIVING US A QUIZ ON GRANDPARENTS DAY!

IT'S ONLY A SHORT TRUE-FALSE QUIZ.
BUT THAT'S NOT FAIR TO ALL THE GRAND-PARENTS!

ARE THEY JUST GOING TO SIT HERE FOR TWENTY MINUTES WHILE WE ANSWER QUESTIONS ABOUT THE CIVIL WAR?

HMM... YOU DO HAVE A POINT.
YES, I DO!

FORTUNATELY, I HAVE ENOUGH COPIES FOR THE GRANDPARENTS TO PARTICIPATE, TOO!

WHAT FUN!
RIGHT.
POINK!
Peirce

ALL RIGHT, CLASS, OPEN YOUR TEXT-BOOKS TO PAGE...
HOLD IT, **HOLD** IT!

IT'S **GRANDPARENTS DAY!** HOW COME WE'RE DOING THE USUAL STUFF? CAN'T WE DO SOMETHING **SPECIAL**, LIKE PLAY A GAME OR WATCH A MOVIE?

I HAVE TOO MUCH RESPECT FOR ALL THE GRANDPARENTS TO CONCOCT SOME SORT OF PHONY ACTIVITY TO MAKE THE CLASS MORE "ENTERTAINING."

SHE'S GOOD.
PERSONALLY, I'D **WELCOME** A PHONY ACTIVITY RIGHT ABOUT NOW.
PEIRCE

THAT'S MY GRAND-FATHER OVER THERE! HE'S A WELL-KNOWN **DOCTOR**!
HM. VERY INTERESTING, GINA.

HE'S CHIEF OF SURGERY AT THE BEST HOSPITAL IN THE STATE! HE'S WON ALL SORTS OF AWARDS! HE'S BEEN ON TELEVISION!

BET MY GRANDFATHER COULD TAKE HIM.
Peirce

THINK YOU COULD TAKE THAT GUY, GRAMPS?
OH YEAH. IN MY SLEEP.

YAWN.. YOUR GRAND-FATHER IS SOME SORT OF MEGA-FAMOUS DOCTOR, EH?
YUP!

WHERE'S YOUR GRANDMOTHER?

!

PROBABLY ROLLING OVER IN HER GRAVE.
OKAY, **NOW** I'M IMPRESSED!
Peirce

THAT'S GINA'S GRAND-FATHER OVER THERE, AND SEE THAT LADY NEXT TO HIM? THAT'S HIS **WIFE**!

SHE MUST BE, LIKE, FORTY YEARS YOUNGER THAN HE IS!
YES, AT **LEAST**! THAT'S... THAT'S...

Peirce

THAT'S VERY, VERY, VERY, VERY, VERY, VERY, VERY, VERY, VERY, VERY, VERY, VERY WRONG.

GRAM AND GRAMPS, THIS IS MR. ROSA!
YOUR GRANDSON IS A VERY TALENTED ARTIST!

YOU CAN SEE SOME OF HIS WORK OVER THERE IN OUR DIS-PLAY AREA!
OOH! SHOW US, NATE!

"HORSE AND RIDER." MY GOODNESS, THIS IS **WONDERFUL**!
NOT **THAT** ONE! MINE'S OVER **HERE**!

"SOCIAL STUDIES TEACHER BEING ATTACKED BY CRAZED PIGEONS."
NOW **THAT'S** ART!
Peirce

I LOVE ALL YOUR ART PROJECTS, SWEETIE!
WE DIDN'T EVEN HAVE ART WHEN I WAS IN SCHOOL!

WE HAD WOOD SHOP WITH MR. MULCAHEY! HE HAD NO CLUE WHAT HE WAS DOING! ALL THE TOOLS WERE IN HORRIBLE CONDITION!

I CAN'T TELL YOU HOW MANY TIMES I WAS ALMOST KILLED IN THAT CLASS!
VERN...
REALLY?

WANT TO SEE A NASTY SCAR?
VERN...
GUYS!
Peirce

NATE! HALLO!
OH, HEY, ARTUR.

GRAM, THIS IS ARTUR.
HELLO!
VERY NICE TO MEETING YOU!

YOU ARE ENJOY GRANDPARENTS DAY?
OH, YES! VERY MUCH!

DID YOU BRING **YOUR** GRANDPARENTS TODAY, ARTUR?
NO. THEY ARE LIVE VERY FAR AWAY.

...SO THERE IS NOBODY FOR ME TO SHOWING AROUND.
WELL, **THAT** DOESN'T SEEM FAIR!

WHAT ABOUT IF I SHOW **YOU** AROUND?
WHY, I'D BE **DELIGHTED**!

ARTUR JUST HIJACKED MY GRANDMA.
I'M OKAY WITH IT, AS LONG AS SHE'S BACK BY SUPPERTIME.
?
PEIRCE

WHAT FUN! I HAVEN'T EATEN A SCHOOL LUNCH IN YEARS!
DON'T GET YOUR HOPES UP, GRAM.

THE FOOD ISN'T VERY GOOD.
OH, I'M SURE IT'S DELICIOUS!
URK!

KOFF! ACK!
GRRNK! HCCH!

I'M FLASHING BACK TO THE MEAT LOAF DURING BASIC AT FORT BENNING.
BUT THAT'S COLESLAW.
Peirce

HOW COME THERE ARE SO MANY MORE GRANDMOTHERS HERE THAN GRANDFATHERS?
BECAUSE MEN DIE EARLIER.

WE MATURE LATER, AND WE DIE EARLIER.

AND IN BETWEEN, ALL YOU DO IS WATCH FOOTBALL.

HE LIKES THE SIDE-LINE REPORT-ERS.
...AND CROSS-WORD PUZZLES! LET'S NOT FORGET THE CROSSWORD PUZZLES!
Peirce

IS IT REALLY TRUE THAT WOMEN LIVE LONGER THAN MEN, GRAMPS?
IT'S A STONE COLD FACT.
LCOME
AND·
ENTS

BUT **WHY**? WHY DO MEN DIE YOUNGER?

VERN, I NEED TO VISIT THE RESTROOM. HOLD MY PURSE.

THERE ARE JUST CERTAIN THINGS THAT AGE YOU.
Peirce

I DON'T THINK I'M GOING TO LIKE GETTING OLD.
DON'T BE SO SURE, NATE!

BEING A SENIOR CITIZEN HAS ITS ADVANTAGES.
LIKE WHAT?

UGLY TIE.
peirce

YOU CAN SAY WHAT-EVER YOU WANT, AND EVERYONE JUST ASSUMES YOU'RE GETTING SENILE!

THIS IS MR. STAPLES, MY MATH TEACHER!
OH, MATH WAS MY **FAVORITE** IN HIGH SCHOOL!

UNFORTUNATELY, IT WAS DIFFICULT FOR A YOUNG WOMAN TO HAVE A CAREER IN MATH BACK THEN.

SO INSTEAD... SIGH... I GOT MARRIED.

I COULD HAVE DONE WITHOUT THE SIGH, MARGE.
OH, VERN! I WAS **SWOONING**!
Peirce

RRRRINNG!
LOOKS LIKE SCHOOL'S OVER!
LET'S GO HOME, NATE!
I CAN'T.

MRS. GODFREY GAVE ME DETENTION, REMEMBER?
OH, THAT'S RIGHT! WELL, HERE YOU GO, SWEETIE...

TAKE THESE ALONG TO KEEP YOU GOING!
THANKS, GRAM!

MOLASSES COOKIES AND A BOOK OF "JUMBLES."
Peirce

WHAT'S THAT, DAD?
A BLOOD-PRESSURE MONITOR!

HIGH BLOOD PRESSURE RUNS IN OUR FAMILY, SO I FIGURED I'D START KEEPING AN EYE ON MINE!

HOW DOES IT WORK?
IT'S BATTERY-POWERED! I JUST HIT THIS BUTTON...
beep!

...AND THE CUFF AUTOMATICALLY INFLATES AND DEFLATES!
WHIRRR
THE NUMBERS ON THE SCREEN ARE GOING DOWN.

YUP! THAT MEANS IT'S WORKING! IT'LL GIVE ME THE FINAL READING IN A FEW SECONDS!
SLAM!

GASP! GASP! GASP!
WHEEEEW!

RRINNG!
DON'T ANSWER THAT!

THE NUMBERS ARE GOING BACK UP.
UH... I MEAN... I'LL GET IT.
Peirce

HM, LET'S SEE WHAT DAD PACKED ME FOR...
WHAT THE...? OH, COME ON!

IS HE SERIOUS? DOES HE ACTUALLY EXPECT ME TO...? OH, GIVE ME A BREAK!

WANNA TRADE LUNCHES?
peirce

CHAD! WANNA TRADE LUNCHES?
MAYBE. WHAT HAVE YOU GOT?

LET'S SEE HERE. UMMMMMMMMMMMM

MMMMMMMMMMMM...

I CAN OFFER YOU SOMETHING IN A LIGHT BROWN.
NO, THANK YOU.
Peirce

DAD, THAT LUNCH YOU PACKED FOR ME TODAY WAS **BRUTAL**.
YOU'RE WELCOME.

IF YOU DIDN'T LIKE IT, WHY DIDN'T YOU TRADE LUNCHES WITH A FRIEND?
I **TRIED** THAT! BUT YOU THINK THAT'S **EASY**?

"HI THERE! WANT TO TRADE YOUR PIZZA AND COOKIES..."

"...FOR A **CELERY STICK** AND A **BEAN SPROUT PITA?**"
DID YOU MENTION THE PITA WAS WHOLE WHEAT?
peirce

HERE, DAD.
WHAT'S THIS?

A LIST OF MY FAV-ORITE FOODS! NOW YOU WON'T WASTE YOUR TIME PACKING LUNCHES I WON'T **EAT**!

YOU FORGOT THE COMMA BETWEEN "CHOCOLATE" AND "BURRITOS."
NO, I DIDN'T!
Peirce

MR. GALVIN, MY DAD KEEPS SENDING ME TO SCHOOL WITH **NASTY** LUNCHES. I HAVEN'T EATEN SINCE BREAKFAST. I'M **STARVING**.
MM-HM.

I DON'T SUPPOSE YOU... HEH HEH!... HAVE ANYTHING EDIBLE IN YOUR DESK?

WELL, LET'S TAKE A LOOK...

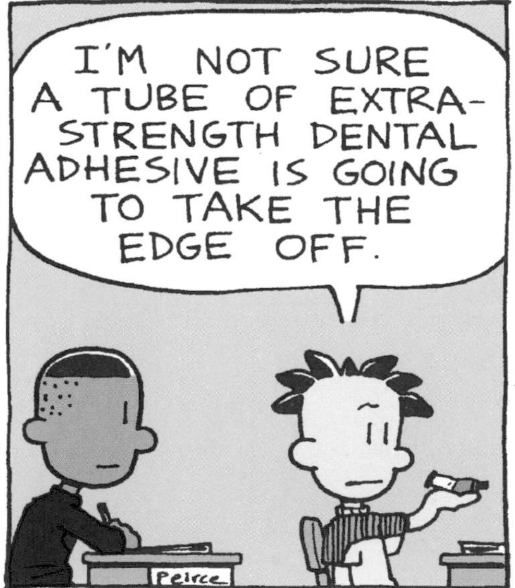
I'M NOT SURE A TUBE OF EXTRA-STRENGTH DENTAL ADHESIVE IS GOING TO TAKE THE EDGE OFF.
Peirce

WHAT IS **THAT**?
AN EXPERIMENT, TEDDY. I'M SICK OF THE HORRIBLE LUNCHES MY DAD MAKES FOR ME.

...SO I TOOK EVERYTHING I COULD FIND IN OUR KITCHEN AND THREW IT ALL TOGETHER IN A PLASTIC BOWL.

NARF!
SLURPF!
SLOSH!
NOSH!

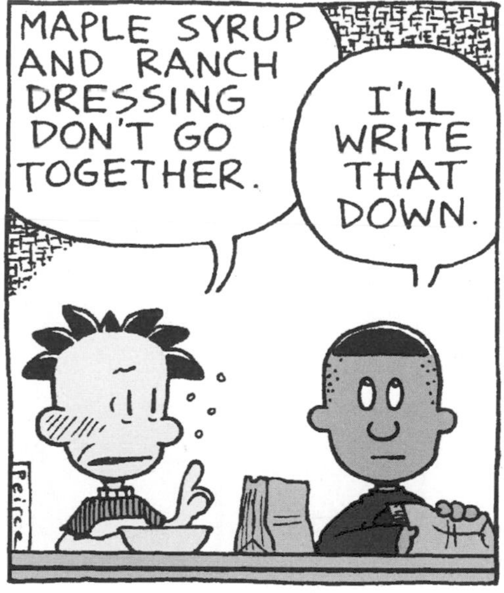
MAPLE SYRUP AND RANCH DRESSING DON'T GO TOGETHER.
I'LL WRITE THAT DOWN.
Peirce

TIME TO SEE HOW MY NEW SWING WORKS!
NEW SWING?
HOLE 1
PAR 4

MY SWING'S ALWAYS BEEN TOO MECH-ANICAL! TOO HERKY-JERKY! SO I'VE CHANGED IT!

MY NEW SWING IS SMOOTHER! MORE GRACEFUL!

THE KEY WORD, NATE, IS "FLUID."
FLUID.

FLUID!

POW!

FLUID.
I THINK IT'S MORE THIS WAY.
Peirce

ALL I NEED IS AN 82 ON THE SOCIAL STUDIES FINAL AND I'LL GET AN A FOR THE SEMESTER!
QUIE
PLEAS

WHAT DO I NEED TO GET AN A?

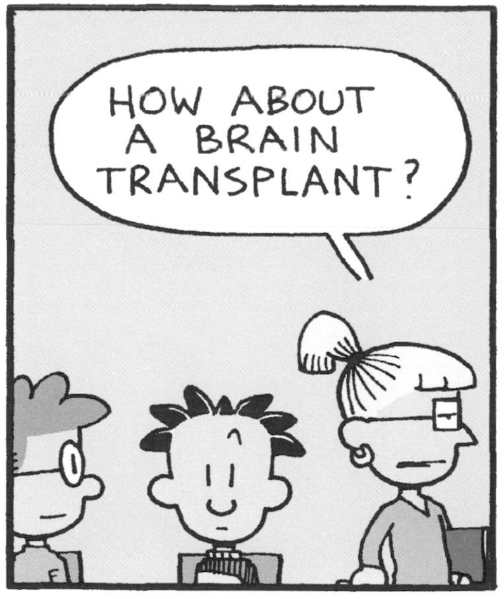
HOW ABOUT A BRAIN TRANSPLANT?

HEH HEH!
NOT THE ANSWER YOU HAD IN MIND?
WHA...?... I... YOU...THAT... OH, YEAH?
peirce

NO MATTER WHAT YOU GET ON THE SOCIAL STUDIES FINAL, NATE, YOU CAN'T GET AN A FOR THE SEMESTER.
NUTS. WHAT DO I NEED TO GET A B?

UMMM... A HUNDRED.
A **HUNDRED**? THAT'S A LITTLE HIGH, FRANCIS.

I MEAN, I WANT A GOOD GRADE AND ALL, BUT I DON'T WANT TO PUT TOO MUCH **PRESSURE** ON MYSELF!

THAT'S NEVER REALLY BEEN A PROBLEM FOR YOU.
HOW 'BOUT A NICE, COMFY C MINUS?
peirce

NATE, IF YOU GET A HUNDRED ON THE SOCIAL STUDIES FINAL, YOU'LL GET A B FOR THE SEMESTER! WHY NOT TRY?
BECAUSE...

BECAUSE HE COULDN'T GET A HUNDRED ON AN EXAM IF HIS LIFE DEPENDED ON IT.
SNORT!

WELL, THAT WASN'T VERY NICE!
GAME ON.
Peirce

SO GINA DOESN'T THINK I CAN GET A HUNDRED ON THE SOCIAL STUDIES FINAL, EH? I'LL SHOW HER!

BUT YOU CAN'T STAND GINA! WHY DO YOU CARE WHAT SHE THINKS?
BECAUSE IT MOTIVATES ME, FRANCIS!

TOM BRADY HATES THE STEELERS, RIGHT? THAT'S WHY HE WANTS TO BEAT THEM SO BAD!

YOU'RE COMPARING YOURSELF TO THE MVP OF THE NFL.
THERE'S NO COMPARISON. I HAVE BETTER HAIR.
Peirce

WANT ME TO HELP YOU STUDY FOR THE SOCIAL STUDIES FINAL?
NO THANKS, FRANCIS. YOU'RE TOO OBSESSIVE-COMPULSIVE.

I AM **NOT**! I JUST LIKE TO BE **ORGAN-IZED**!
LAST TIME, YOU REWROTE ALL YOUR CLASS NOTES.

SO? **LOTS** OF PEOPLE REWRITE THEIR NOTES BEFORE A TEST!
YOU DID IT SEVENTEEN TIMES.

I WASN'T HAPPY WITH THE TEXT-TO-MARGINS RATIO THE FIRST SIXTEEN TIMES.
UH-HUH.
Peirce

SO NATE THINKS HE CAN GET A HUNDRED ON THE SOCIAL STUDIES FINAL?
HE'LL NEED SOME HELP, THAT'S FOR SURE.

ARE YOU GOING TO TUTOR HIM?
I OFFERED, BUT HE SAID NO.

I GUESS HE'S GOT ANOTHER TUTOR IN MIND.

MEANWHILE...
PETER, M'BOY!
OH, NO.
Peirce

PENNY FOR YOUR THOUGHTS!
A **PENNY**? *SNORT!* I DON'T **THINK** SO!

IT'S JUST AN **EXPRESSION**, PINHEAD!
WELL, MY THOUGHTS ARE WORTH AT **LEAST** A **DOLLAR**!

A **DOLLAR**? FOR**GET** IT!
FINE. YOUR LOSS.

HMMM...
HEH HEH!...
OOOOOH!
AH **HA**!

TOO BAD YOU'RE MISSING OUT ON ALL THESE **THOUGHTS**, FRANCIS! THERE'S SOME GREAT STUFF IN HERE! STUFF THAT YOU MIGHT FIND
OKAY, O**KAY**!

HERE'S A BUCK. WHAT ARE YOUR THOUGHTS?
I'LL WRITE 'EM DOWN!

HERE YOU GO!
RRIP!

Sucker!
Peirce

PETER! WANNA HELP ME STUDY FOR MY SOCIAL STUDIES FINAL?
ME? I'M ONLY IN **FIRSHT GRADE**!

YEAH, BUT YOU'RE SMARTER THAN MOST **COLLEGE PROFESSORS**!
HMM... YESH, THAT'SH TRUE...

...AND I **DO** FIND SHOCIAL SHTUDIES ESHPECIALLY SHCINTILLATING!

WHERE SHALL WE SHTART?
HOW ABOUT WITH A TOWEL?
Peirce

IF WE'RE GOING TO SHTUDY FOR YOUR FINAL, WE NEED TO SHTART WITH YOUR CLASSH NOTESH.
GOTCHA. HERE.

ONE PAGE? WHERE'SH THE RESHT OF IT?
WHATTA YA MEAN?

WE NEED YOUR NOTESH FOR THE WHOLE **YEAR**.
THOSE **ARE** MY NOTES FOR THE WHOLE YEAR.

CRIPESH.
DID I MENTION I DON'T LIKE SOCIAL STUDIES VERY MUCH?
Peirce

YOUR SHO-CALLED **NOTESH** ARE A COMPLETE **JOKE**!
OKAY, SO I'M NOT GREAT AT TAKING NOTES! THERE'S NO NEED TO BE **RUDE**!

YOU KNOW, PETER, MOST FIRST-GRADERS WOULD TREAT A SIXTH-GRADER WITH A LITTLE MORE **RESPECT**!

MOSHT SHIXTH-GRADERSH WOULDN'T ASHK A FIRSHT-GRADER TO BE THEIR TUTOR.

TOUCHÉ.
...WHICH REMINDSH ME, WE SHOULD DISCUSSH MY FEE.
Peirce

OKAY, I'M GOING TO QUIZ YOU. I'LL GIVE YOU AN EVENT, AND YOU TELL ME THE DATE.
PIECE O' CAKE!

GETTYSHBURG ADDRESSH.
JUNE 23RD, 2011!

YOU CAN'T POSSHIBLY BE THISH SHTUPID.
THE 22ND? NO! THE 24TH!
Peirce

GIVE IT TO ME STRAIGHT, PETER: WHAT ARE MY CHANCES OF GETTING A HUNDRED ON MY SOCIAL STUDIES FINAL?

ROUGHLY THE EQUIV-ALENT OF CUSHTER'SH CHANCESH AT THE LITTLE BIGHORN.

YES!

...RIGHT?
TELL YOU WHAT, LET'SH REVIEW CHAPTER TWELVE.
U.S. HISTORY
Peirce

PRESHIDENT OF THE CONFEDERACY?
JEFFERSON DAVIS.
BATTLE OF ANTIETAM?
SEPTEMBER 17TH, 1862.

LINCOLN'SH SHECRETARY OF THE NAVY?
GIDEON WELLES.
DRED SHCOTT DECISHION?
MARCH 6TH, 1857.
WHO TOOK ATLANTA?
WILLIAM TECUMSEH SHERMAN.

WHO WASH IMPEACHED IN 1868?
ANDREW JOHNSON.
WHAT FOR?
VIOLATION OF THE TENURE OF OFFICE ACT.

I DON'T EVEN **KNOW** YOU ANYMORE!
WHEW!
Peirce

YOU'RE ON DECK, NATE! GRAB A BAT!
RIGHT, COACH!
CLAP CLAP

WANT A QUICK SCOUTING REPORT ON THE PITCHER?
NO.

WHY NOT?
BECAUSE YOU DRIVE ME **NUTS** WITH ALL YOUR STUPID STATS AND SABER-METRICS, FRANCIS!

WHAT'S **THIS** GUY'S E.R.A. AGAINST PINCH HITTERS ON THURSDAYS? WHAT'S **THAT** GUY'S W.H.I.P. IN ODD-NUMBERED INNINGS? WHO **CARES**?

THAT STUFF MEANS NOTHING IN THE BATTER'S BOX! IF YOU WANT TO GIVE ME A SCOUTING REPORT, MAKE IT INFORMATION I CAN **USE!**

DOOF!

I WAS GOING TO MENTION THAT HE'S A LITTLE WILD.
Peirce

READY FOR THE SOCIAL STUDIES FINAL?
YUP! READY TO GET A **HUNDRED**!
OH, **PLEASE**!

YOU'LL BE LUCKY TO **PASS**!
PASS? OH, I'LL PASS, GINA...

...JUST LIKE THE SHERMAN ANTITRUST ACT, WHICH PASSED ON JULY 2ND, 1890, MARKING THE BEGINNING OF THE GOVERNMENT'S EFFORT TO RESTRICT MONOPOLIES.

WHA...?
SO SHUT UP.
Peirce

WOW. THIS IS THE EASIEST TEST I'VE EVER TAKEN IN MY **LIFE**!

I KNOW EVERY ANSWER! I MEAN, I DON'T **THINK** I KNOW... I **KNOW** I KNOW! I'M ONE HUNDRED PERCENT **POSITIVE**!

...AND ALL BECAUSE I **STUDIED**!

HOW SICKENING.
Peirce

BEFORE YOU LEAVE FOR THE SUMMER, PEOPLE, I'M PASSING BACK YOUR FINAL EXAMS.
AH! GET READY, GINA!

YOU SAID I WASN'T CAPABLE OF GETTING A HUNDRED ON THE FINAL! WELL, PREPARE TO BE W-R-O-N-G!

EXCELLENT JOB, NATE.
HEAR THAT, GINA? "EXCELLENT JOB"!

GAWK!
PEIRCE

LOOKS LIKE YOU **DIDN'T** GET A HUNDRED ON THE FINAL, EINSTEIN!
A 99?

MRS. GODFREY, WHY DID I GET A 99 ON THE FINAL? I GOT EVERYTHING **RIGHT**!

YOU DIDN'T WRITE YOUR NAME IN THE SPACE PROVIDED. THAT'S AN AUTOMATIC ONE-POINT DEDUCTION.

OH, HOW I HATE HER.
WANT TO SEE WHAT A **REAL** HUNDRED LOOKS LIKE?
peirce

MRS. GODFREY, I NEEDED A HUNDRED ON THE FINAL TO GET A B FOR THE SEMESTER.
UH HUH...

WELL, SINCE I CAME SO CLOSE – Y'KNOW, GETTING A 99 AND EVERYTHING – DO YOU THINK MAYBE YOU COULD GIVE ME A B ANYWAY?

WHY WOULD I DO THAT?

BECAUSE YOU'RE SO STINKIN' NICE!
HAVE A GOOD SUMMER.
Peirce

I CAN'T BELIEVE MRS. GODFREY GAVE ME A 99 INSTEAD OF A HUNDRED! WHAT A JERK!

YOU KNOW WHAT I HOPE? I HOPE SHE GOES ON SAFARI THIS SUMMER AT SOME SORT OF AFRICAN GAME PRESERVE!...

...AND THEN SHE WANDERS OFF ALONE AND GETS ATTACKED BY A CRAZED WILDEBEEST!

THEN, AS SHE STAGGERS BACK TO THE TOUR BUS, THE HYENAS MOVE IN...
HE GETS VERY CREATIVE WITH HIS REVENGE FANTASIES.
PEIRCE

AHHH, SUMMER!
HEY! I JUST THOUGHT OF SOME-THING!

WE WERE SO BUSY CRAMMING FOR FINALS, WE TOTALLY FORGOT ABOUT PRANK DAY!
OH NO!

I HAD SO MANY GREAT PRANKS PLANNED!
TOO LATE NOW. SCHOOL'S OVER.

ARRGH! WHAT WERE WE THINKING?
HEY, HERE'S AN IDEA!

WE'LL SPEND ALL SUMMER PLANNING SOME AWESOME PRANKS FOR THE FIRST DAY OF SCHOOL IN SEPTEMBER!

YESS! LET'S DO IT!
SHAKE ON IT!

BZZZZZ

FOOOSH

YANK!
Peirce

HI, WE'RE HERE FOR THE JUNIOR LIFE-SAVING CLASS.
THAT WAY.
STAF
RACK
POO

I CAN'T BELIEVE MY PARENTS ARE MAKING ME DO THIS.
MAYBE IT WON'T BE SO BAD, TEDDY!

MAYBE OUR INSTRUCTOR WILL BE A TURBO HOTTIE WHO'S, LIKE, HALF LIFEGUARD, HALF **SUPERMODEL**!

AWRIGHT, SCRUBS, GET READY TO **SAVE SOME LIVES**!
COACH JOHN!
!
!
Peirce

COACH JOHN! **YOU'RE** OUR JUNIOR LIFESAVING INSTRUCTOR?
WHAT WERE YOU **EXPECTING,** JUNIOR?

SOME BLOW-DRIED COLLEGE KID WITH A **SPRAY TAN,** RUNNING DOWN THE BEACH IN **SLOW MOTION**?

WATER SAFETY ISN'T A **TV SHOW**, SON! BEING A LIFEGUARD ISN'T ALL **GLAMOUR**!

I THINK I REALIZED IT WASN'T ALL GLAMOUR WHEN I SAW COACH JOHN IN HIS SPEEDO.
HE'S GOT THE SLOW MOTION PART DOWN.
Peirce

AWRIGHT, TROOPS, TIME TO SEE IF YOU'VE GOT WHAT IT TAKES TO BE **JUNIOR LIFESAVERS!**

GET YOURSELVES INTO THE POOL, AND...

WAHOOOO

CARE TO TRY THAT AGAIN, JUNIOR?
NO RUNNING
NO DIVING
HM?
Peirce

IS IT REALLY NECESSARY TO SLANDER A LEGENDARY SNACK FOOD?

POOL PARTY? THE ONLY POOLS IN OUR NEIGHBORHOOD ARE INFLATABLE!

Peirce

PUT THESE ON, THEN GET IN THE WATER.
HUH? WHY ARE WE PUTTING ON CLOTHES FROM THE LOST & FOUND?

BECAUSE IF YOU FALL OFF A **BOAT**, YOU HAVE TO BE ABLE TO **INFLATE** YOUR CLOTHES TO KEEP YOURSELF **AFLOAT**!

WHA-?... THIS IS A **YANKEES** SHIRT! I'M A **RED SOX** FAN! I CAN'T WEAR **THIS**!
6F

I'D RATHER DROWN.
TRADE YA.
Barbie
Peirce

A JUNIOR LIFESAVER NEEDS TO BE ABLE TO TREAD WATER FOR EXTENDED PERIODS OF TIME! SO **STAY IN THE POOL** UNTIL I TELL YOU TO COME OUT!
AWWW!
BUT IT'S **COLD!**

NO COMPLAINING! I DON'T WANT TO HEAR A **PEEP** OUT OF YOU UNLESS IT'S AN **EMERGENCY! GOT IT?**

MY FINGERS ARE GETTING ALL PRUNEY.
CHAD! SSSHH!
Peirce

ARTUR! WANNA PLAY KICK THE CAN?
KICK THE CAN? HOKAY!

WHERE I SHOULD KICK IT?
YOU CAN'T KICK IT YET, ARTUR!

OF COURSE! BECAUSE I DO NOT KNOW WHERE IS THE GOAL!
NO, NO... THERE ARE NO GOALS IN KICK THE CAN!

THERE'S LIKE A HOME BASE, AND...
AH! HOME BASE! SO IS LIKE BASEBALL!

NO, IT'S NOT! ONE PERSON IS IT, SEE...
WHAT "IT" IS?

THAT'S THE PERSON WHO HAS TO FIND EVERYBODY!
OH HO! I CAN FIND EVERYBODY! THEY ARE OVER THERE!

I AM GOOD AT THIS GAME!
CLANNG!!
Peirce

TEDDY! GRAB YOUR STUFF! WE'VE GOT TO GET TO THE POOL!
I'M NOT GOING TODAY. I'M SICK.

WHAT? BUT WE'RE **PARTNERS**! I CAN'T PRACTICE LIFESAVING TECHNIQUES BY MY**SELF**!
YEAH, I KNOW. SORRY ABOUT THAT, DUDE.

I'M SURE COACH JOHN WILL FIGURE OUT A WAY TO KEEP YOU BUSY.

GULP.

Peirce

SIMULATED **RESCUE** TIME, SOLDIERS!
YOU AND YOUR PARTNERS WILL TAKE TURNS RESCUING EACH OTHER!

CHOP **CHOP**, JUNIOR! LOOK ALIVE! WHERE'S YOUR PARTNER?
UH... HE'S SICK TODAY.
CLAP
CLAP

SO I GUESS I'LL JUST SIT OVER HERE AND WATCH.

NICE TRY, SONNY. **I'LL** BE YOUR PARTNER.
NO. NO. NO. NO. NO.
Peirce

OKAY, KID, INTO THE WATER. I'LL PRETEND TO BE DROWNING, AND YOU PULL ME TO SHORE.
UH... OKAY, I'LL TRY.

YOU'LL **TRY**? LISTEN, CHAMP, IF YOU WANT TO BE A JUNIOR LIFESAVER, YOU CAN'T JUST **TRY**! YOU'VE GOT TO **DO**!

AND BESIDES, IT WON'T BE AS TOUGH TO RESCUE ME AS YOU THINK.

FOR SOME REASON, I'M UNUSUALLY BUOYANT.
Peirce

NICELY DONE, CHAMP! YOU SUCCESSFULLY PULLED ME TO SAFETY! NOW LET'S GO TO ROUND TWO!
ROUND TWO? I'VE GOTTA DO IT AGAIN?
2 FT

OF COURSE! THE FIRST TIME WAS EASY! I DIDN'T STRUGGLE! I DIDN'T THRASH AROUND LIKE A CRAZED ANIMAL!

THIS TIME, I'LL PRETEND TO BE A SWIMMER IN A FULL-BLOWN PANIC!

KNOW ANYTHING ABOUT PANIC?
I'M STARTING TO.
OKAY, BAYWATCH! COME AND GET ME!
SPLASH!
SPLOOSH!
2 FT

OKAY, KID, I'M AN EX-HAUSTED SWIMMER, AND YOU'RE WITHOUT A FLOTATION DEVICE. WHAT DO YOU DO?
UM... A CROSS-CHEST CARRY?

WELL, THEN, GO AHEAD! WHAT ARE YOU WAITING FOR?
I... I'M **TRYING**, BUT... I CAN'T GET A GOOD HOLD!

TRY **HARDER**, JUNIOR! YOU CAN'T **DILLYDALLY** WHEN IT COMES TO WATER SAFETY! JUST **GRAB** SOMETHING!

ONE SECOND LATER...
NOT THE HAIR, BOY.
OOPS.
Peirce

THANKS A **LOT**, TEDDY! YOU SKIP JUNIOR LIFESAVING, AND I GET STUCK WITH **COACH JOHN** AS MY PARTNER!

I WAS TRYING TO DO A WATER RESCUE, AND I ACCIDENTALLY PULLED HIS **TOUPEE** OFF!

WAIT. COACH JOHN WEARS A **TOUPEE**?
peirce

CHAD, CHAD, CHAD.
MY UNCLE PEDRO CALLS HIS A "HAIR RESTORATION SYSTEM."

SEE THOSE SQUIRRELS OVER THERE, SPITSY? GO GET 'EM!
WHINE!

GO ON, SPITSY! THERE'S NOTHING TO BE AFRAID OF!
WHIMPER!

THEY'RE SQUIRRELS! YOU'RE A DOG! THEY'RE SMALL! YOU'RE BIG!
WURF?

AS SOON AS THEY SEE YOU, THEY'LL RUN AWAY! THAT'S WHAT SQUIRRELS DO!
WORF!

IT'LL BE FUN! I PROMISE! TRUST ME!
WUFF!

WOOF!
WOOF!
WURF!
WURF?
GRRF?
WHIMPER!

WURF?
GRRF?
WHIMPER!
OWOOOO!...

MY BAD.
NYUK! NYUK! NYUK!
Peirce

SOMETHING SMELLS GOOD.
OOH! FRANCIS! ARE THOSE YOUR MOM'S LEMON SQUARES?

YUP! I'M IN CHARGE OF SNACKS THIS WEEK FOR MY BOOK CLUB!
BOOK CLUB?

SO WHOEVER'S IN THE BOOK CLUB GETS TO EAT LEMON SQUARES?
CAN **WE** COME?

UM... WELL, IF YOU HAVEN'T READ THE BOOK, YOU WON'T BE ABLE TO CONTRIBUTE MUCH TO THE DISCUSSION.
PERFECT!
OOH! POWDERED SUGAR!
Peirce

THIS IS WHERE THE BOOK CLUB MEETING IS? THE LIBRARY?
WELL, WHAT'D YOU EXPECT?

I WAS HOPING IT WOULD BE IN SOME LITTLE COFFEE SHOP OR SOMETHING!
...OR EVEN OUTSIDE!

LIBRARIES CAN BE SUCH A DRAG! THEY'RE ALWAYS ALL "QUIET, PLEASE" AND "NO TALKING"!

PLUS, THEY'RE ALWAYS TRYING TO GET YOU TO READ!
YEAH, THEY'RE SO PUSHY!
peirce

HELLO, FRANCIS!
HI, MRS. KILEY! I BROUGHT MY FRIENDS NATE AND TEDDY!

HELLO, BOYS! WILL YOU BE JOINING US IN THE BOOK CLUB FROM NOW ON?
UH... THAT DEPENDS ON WHAT HAP-PENS NEXT WEEK.

WELL, WE'RE GOING TO START READING A **WONDERFUL** NOVEL ABOUT A...
I WAS TALKING ABOUT THE **SNACK** NEXT WEEK.

AH.
ANYTHING CHOCOLATE, AND I'M IN!
BUT NO WAL-NUTS. I HATE WALNUTS.
Peirce

WHAT THE...? OH, **NO**!
OH, **YES**, GINA! TEDDY AND I HAVE JOINED THE BOOK CLUB!

WHY, TO MEET **GIRLS**?
WHATTA YA MEAN?

THE CLUB IS, LIKE, NINETY PERCENT **FEMALE**, PINHEAD!
REALLY?
I DON'T SEE ANY FEMALES AROUND HERE.

WHAT DO YOU THINK I AM?
DON'T ANSWER. IT'S A TRICK QUESTION.
Peirce

WHY DID YOU HAVE TO SHOW UP AT BOOK CLUB? YOU'LL RUIN EVERYTHING!
ME?

YES, YOU! YOU'LL MAKE FUN OF THE BOOK WE'RE READING!
HOW CAN I? I DON'T EVEN KNOW WHAT IT IS!

LOOK, GINA, I CAME FOR THE SNACKS! I'M NOT GOING TO MESS UP YOUR PREC-IOUS LITTLE MEETING! YOU WON'T EVEN KNOW I'M HERE!

LET'S RESUME OUR DISCUSSION OF "ANIMAL FARM."
NARF!
SLURP!
CHOMP!
NARF
NARF
GULP
NYULP.
Peirce

I'M PASSING OUT COPIES OF OUR NEXT BOOK: "LORD OF THE FLIES."
OH HO!

IS IT ABOUT A MAD SCIENTIST WHO ACCIDENTALLY TURNS HIMSELF INTO AN INSECT?

NO, IT IS NOT.
OH.

ARE THERE ANY OTHER QUESTIONS?
BASEBALL?
Peirce

I THINK HE IS. I REALLY DO.
FREAKY.
WHAT'S FREAKY?

WE THINK THAT GUY OVER THERE MIGHT BE DEAD.
WHAT? OH, COME ON! HE'S PROBABLY JUST ASLEEP!

NO, FRANCIS! TEDDY AND I HAVE BEEN WATCHING HIM FOR AN HOUR!
HE HASN'T MOVED ONCE! I DON'T THINK HE'S BREATHING!

WELL, SHOULDN'T WE TELL A LIFEGUARD OR SOMETHING?
I THINK FIRST WE NEED TO FIND OUT FOR SURE IF HE'S DEAD.

I KNOW! I'LL HUCK A FRISBEE OVER THERE, AND WHEN I GO GET IT, I'LL BE CLOSE ENOUGH TO GET A GOOD LOOK AT THE GUY!

ZING!

THROW THAT THING NEAR ME AGAIN, AND IT'LL BE THE LAST THING YOU'LL EVER THROW.
Peirce

NOT ONLY IS HE ALIVE, I THINK I MIGHT HAVE SEEN HIM LAST WEEK ON "AMERICA'S MOST WANTED."

YOU DON'T LOOK SO GOOD, NATE.
I WAS HAVING A SNACK, AND I STARTED FEELING SICK.

A SNACK?... GOOD GRAVY! DID YOU EAT THIS ENTIRE BAG OF CHEEZ DOODLES?
UH... YEAH.

THAT'S WHY YOU'RE SICK, NATE! YOU ATE WAY TOO MUCH JUNK FOOD!
CHEEZ DOODLES

IT'S TIME FOR YOU TO CUT BACK ON THE CHEEZ DOODLES.
NO!
Peirce

UH... DAD, WHAT DO YOU MEAN, I HAVE TO CUT BACK ON CHEEZ DOODLES?
YOU EAT TOO MANY OF THEM, THAT'S WHAT I MEAN!

THIS BAG YOU JUST ATE IN ONE SITTING CONTAINS **FIFTEEN SERVINGS!** A BAG THIS SIZE SHOULD LAST FOR OVER **TWO WEEKS!**
CHEEZ DOODLES

HA HA HA HA HA HA HA HA HEH HEH HEH...
DOODLES

IT'S NEVER GOOD TO BE THE ONLY ONE LAUGHING.
"DOODLES PER SERVING: 6.5"
Peirce

SO YOU'RE SAYING THIS BAG OF CHEEZ DOODLES SHOULD LAST **TWO WEEKS**?
UH-HUH. IF YOU EAT ONE SERVING A DAY.

BUT IF YOU KEEP CHEEZ DOODLES AROUND THAT LONG, THEY GET **STALE!** THEN YOU'VE GOT TO THROW THEM **AWAY!** THAT'S **WASTEFUL!**

DO YOU WANT ME TO THROW AWAY CHEEZ DOODLES SO THAT THEY POLLUTE OUR WATER AND CLOG OUR LAND-FILLS?

SO BY EATING CHEEZ DOODLES, YOU'RE ACTUALLY HELPING THE ENVIRONMENT.
YES! **YES!** I'M AN **ECO-WARRIOR!**

OKAY, NATE, HERE'S 6.5 CHEEZ DOODLES. THAT'S ONE SERVING. MAKE IT LAST ALL DAY.
ALL DAY?

THAT'S IMPOSSIBLE!! I CAN'T SURVIVE ON THIS! I'LL STARVE!

SIIIGH..

IS THERE ANYTHING MORE PATHETIC THAN HALF A CHEEZ DOODLE?
I CAN THINK OF SOME-THING.
peirce

HOW AM I GOING TO MAKE THESE CHEEZ DOODLES LAST ALL DAY?
JUST IGNORE THEM.

IGNORE THEM. IGNORE THEM. IGNORE THEM. IGNORE THEM.

NARF NARF NUMPF NOMMPF CHOMPF CHOMF NARMF, NUMPF

OUT OF SIGHT, OUT OF MIND.
Peirce

HOW GOES IT?
I ATE MY DAILY ALLOWANCE OF CHEEZ DOODLES. NOW I CAN'T HAVE MORE UNTIL TOMORROW.

I DON'T THINK I CAN MAKE IT.... IF I CAN'T EAT ANY CHEEZ DOODLES, I MIGHT... I'LL... I...

EW. YOU'VE GOT ORANGE POWDER ALL OVER YOUR SHIRT.
I DO? I DO!

THIS MAY BE MORE SERIOUS THAN I REALIZED.
SUCK
SUCK
SUCK
SUCK
SUCK
SUCK
Peirce

A METAL DETECTOR?
I BORROWED IT FROM MY GRANDFATHER!

HE SAYS THE BEACH IS THE BEST PLACE TO FIND COINS AND JEWELRY AND STUFF!

LIKE BURIED TREASURE!
EXACTLY! I'LL JUST TURN IT ON, AND...
KLIK!

OOP! GUESS WHAT! IT'S DETECTING SOMETHING **ALREADY**!
boop
boop

SO LONG, TEDDY! THE NEXT TIME YOU SEE ME, I MIGHT BE **RICH**!
boop
boop
boop

!

SORRY SORRY SORRY SORRY

EITHER THIS THING DOESN'T WORK, OR THAT LADY HAS A STEEL PLATE IN HER HEAD.
Peirce

HI, NATE. WHAT'S THE MATTER?
MY DAD'S STARVING ME TO DEATH, CHAD.

HE'S MAKING ME LIMIT MY CHEEZ DOODLE INTAKE.
SO YOU'RE DIETING?

WELL... YEAH, I GUESS.
HEY, MY GRAMMY JUST PUT **ME** ON A DIET, **TOO**! WE CAN DIET **TOGETHER**!

WORST SUMMER EVER.
CELERY?
Peirce

"ONE SERVING PER DAY."

I'M SUPPOSED TO LIVE ON THAT?

HA! I DON'T **THINK** SO!
Peirce

NARF NARF NARF NARF
NARF NARF NARF NARF
NARF NARF NARF
NARF NARF
NARF NARF
NARF NARF
NARF NARF
CHEEZ DOODLE HAIKU

AGGH! I DROPPED MY CHEEZ DOODLES IN THE **SAND**!
SO THROW 'EM AWAY.

I **CAN'T**! I'M ONLY ALLOWED ONE SERVING PER DAY! THESE ARE ALL I **HAVE**!

WASH 'EM OFF, THEN.
YOU CAN'T **WASH** CHEEZ DOODLES, FRANCIS! THEY'LL GET ALL **SOGGY**!

WELL, YOU CERTAINLY CAN'T **EAT** THEM LIKE...
CRONCH! CRACK! KKRRCH!
Peirce

WOOP WOOP
WOOP WOOP
WOOP WOOP

WHAT KIND OF PSYCHO DAD INSTALLS AN ALARM IN THE SNACK CABINET?
NICE HAIR.
SPORTS
Peirce

GREAT NEWS, NATE! I'VE SOLVED THE CHEEZ DOODLE PROBLEM!
"CHEEZY WEEZIES"?

THEY'RE EXACTLY LIKE CHEEZ DOODLES, BUT THEY'RE **LOW-FAT!** YOU CAN EAT THEM TO YOUR HEART'S CONTENT!
MUNCH MUNCH

THEY'RE PUFFY! THEY'RE CRUNCHY! THEY'RE SAVORY! THEY'RE...UH...
OOLP!

THEY'RE ORANGE...
THIS IS LIKE PROMISING A KID A PUPPY, THEN COMING HOME WITH A SCOOBY-DOO HAND PUPPET.
Peirce

DAD, YOU'D NEVER MAKE ME DO ANY-THING YOU WOULDN'T BE WILLING TO DO YOURSELF, RIGHT?
UH... RIGHT.

WELL, IF **I** HAVE TO CUT BACK ON EATING CHEEZ DOODLES, **YOU** SHOULD HAVE TO CUT BACK ON **ICE CREAM!**

ME?... *KOFF!* I DON'T EAT ALL THAT MUCH ICE CREAM.
OH YEAH? LET'S EX-AMINE THE RECYCLING BIN!

BUSTED.
...OR AS **I** LIKE TO CALL IT, THE "BEN & JERRY'S GRAVE-YARD!
CARDBOARD
Peirce

DANG! I FORGOT MY RADIO!

NOW I CAN'T KEEP TABS ON THE RED SOX GAME!
HEY, IT'S A BIG BEACH.

IT SHOULD BE EASY TO FIND SOMEONE WITH A RADIO!
MAYBE **THAT** GUY'S LISTENING TO THE GAME!

YEAH, OR MAYBE HE'S LISTENING TO **FUSION JAZZ**!
OOP! LOOK!

HE'S DOING A **FIST PUMP!**
YESSSS!

SO I GUESS HE'S **NOT** LISTENING TO FUSION JAZZ!
YOU'RE **RIGHT,** TEDDY! HE **MUST** HAVE THE GAME ON!

NOW I'LL FIND OUT WHAT THAT **FIST PUMP** MEANT!

IT MEANS HE'S A YANKEES FAN.

NOW, FOR A LOOK AT THE WEATHER, HERE'S CHIEF METEOROLOGIST CHIP CAVENDISH!
WAIT, WHAT? WHO?

WHO'S THIS YAHOO? WHERE'S WINK SUMMERS?
ON VACATION, PROBABLY.

BUT THEY JUST CALLED THIS GUY THE "CHIEF METEOROLOGIST"! WINK IS THE CHIEF METEOROLOGIST!
WELL, THEN, IT MUST BE SOMETHING ELSE.

SOMETHING ELSE?
...AND THE STORM CLOUDS GATHER.
Peirce

THIS IS AN **OUTRAGE**! WHY IS **THIS** CLOWN DOING THE WEATHER INSTEAD OF WINK SUMMERS?
WHY DOES IT MATTER?

DAD! IT **MATTERS** BECAUSE WINK'S MY FAVORITE LOCAL TV PERSONALITY! **THIS** GUY IS A TOTAL **STIFF**!

HE CAN'T BANTER WITH THE CO-ANCHORS LIKE **WINK** CAN!

BANTER BANTER BANTER BANTER BANTER BANTER
BONK!
OW!
SEE?
peirce

ELLEN! GO TO CHANNEL 12'S WEBSITE!
WHAT FOR?

I NEED TO SEE WHAT HAPPENED TO WINK SUMMERS! HURRY **UP**!
O**KAY**, OKAY! KEEP YOUR SHIRT ON!

IS THERE ANYTHING THERE? WHAT'S IT SAY?
"FORMER CHIEF METEOR-OLOGIST WINK SUMMERS..."

"FORMER"?
peirce

WHAT'S ALL THE FUSS?
CHANNEL 12 IS TURNING WINK SUMMERS INTO THE **WEEKEND** WEATHER GUY!

WHAT ARE THEY **THINKING**? THAT'S A **DEMOTION**! THAT'S LIKE SENDING ALBERT PUJOLS TO THE **MINORS**!

OOP. WAIT, IT SAYS THAT ACCORDING TO THE STATION MAN-AGER, THIS WAS A **MUTUAL DECISION**!

...SO MAYBE THIS IS WHAT WINK **WANTED**!
SON, LET ME EXPLAIN WHAT "MUTUAL DECISION" MEANS IN THE REAL WORLD...
Peirce

HELLO, IS THIS CHANNEL 12 METEOROLOGIST WINK SUMMERS?... WINK!... NATE WRIGHT HERE!

LISTEN, WINK, I JUST WANT TO TELL YOU IT STINKS THAT THE STATION DEMOTED YOU TO WEEKENDS! THIS GUY WHO'S TAKING YOUR PLACE IS AWFUL!

HE'S LIKE A KEN DOLL! HE'S SO FAKE! HE DOESN'T HAVE ANY OF YOUR CLUMSY, OVERWEIGHT, AVERAGE JOE CHARM!

HELLO?... WINK?... HELLO?
Peirce

POOR WINK SUMMERS. HE **WAS** CHANNEL 12'S CHIEF METEOROLOGIST. NOW HE'S ONLY THE **WEEKEND** GUY. HE MUST BE SO BUMMED OUT.

BUT HE'S **STILL** GOING TO SUCK IT UP AND GIVE THE BEST FORECAST HE CAN! THE MAN HAS **PRIDE**! HE'S A **PRO**!

IT MIGHT RAIN TOMORROW... OR IT MIGHT NOT. HOW SHOULD **I** KNOW? WHO EVEN **CARES**?

BACK TO YOU, SUSAN.
THERE MAY BE A SHORT ADJUSTMENT PERIOD.
Peirce

YOU COMING?
ARRGH! I LEFT MY PASS AT HOME!
NICNACK BEACH
STATE PARK
ADULTS 5
CHILDREN...... 3
OR SHOW SEASON PASS

CAN I GO IN WITHOUT A PASS, MISTER? JUST THIS ONCE?
'FRAID NOT. SORRY.

CAN YOU PAY YOUR WAY IN?
WELL... I COULD USE MY SNACK MONEY...

... BUT I **DO** HAVE A PASS, MISTER! I USE IT ALL THE **TIME!** DON'T YOU REMEMBER ME?
NICNACK BEACH
STATE PARK
OR SHOW SEASON PASS

HUNDREDS OF PEOPLE COME THROUGH HERE EVERY DAY, SON. YOU'RE JUST ANOTHER KID.

HMMPH!

SIIIGH

IT'S NOT ABOUT THE MONEY.
JUST ANOTHER KID.
Peirce

OOH, YARD SALE! LET'S CHECK IT OUT, FRANCIS!
WHY?...

SO YOU CAN BUY SOME PIECE OF JUNK THAT YOU'RE CRAZY ENOUGH TO THINK IS WORTH A LOT OF MONEY?
HA! CRAZY LIKE A FOX!

I'M A VISIONARY! UNLIKE YOU, I CAN SEE WHEN STUFF HAS VALUE! I THINK OUTSIDE THE BOX!

...AND SPEAKING OF BOXES, HERE'S A CARDBOARD ONE FOR ONLY FIFTY CENTS!
OOH! IS THE CARD-BOARD IN MINT CONDITION?

CAN WE LEAVE NOW? YOU'RE **NOT** GOING TO FIND SOME PRICE-LESS ANTIQUE IN THE MIDDLE OF ALL THIS...
OH **HO**!

YOU SPOKE TOO **SOON**, FRANCIS! LOOK AT **THIS** LITTLE ITEM! A MINIATURE SILVER **SCULPTURE**!

NOTE THE FINE CRAFTSMANSHIP! THE ATTENTION TO DETAIL! MY EAGLE EYE MIGHT HAVE JUST SPOTTED A **DIAMOND IN THE ROUGH**!

THAT'S A "WIMPY KID" PENCIL SHARPENER.
EX**ACTLY**! IT'S A **CLASSIC**!
Peirce

C'MON, LET'S GO. I TOLD TEDDY WE'D...
WHOA, FRANCIS! HOLD EVERY-THING!
ARD
ALE

LOOK AT THIS! A CAPTAIN VOLTAGE FIGURINE! I SAW ONE OF THESE FOR SALE AT "KLASSIC KOMIX" FOR A HUNDRED BUCKS!

... AND THIS GUY'S SELLING IT FOR TEN! HE DOESN'T REALIZE WHAT IT'S WORTH! HE HAS NO CLUE!

SEE ANYTHING YOU LIKE, BOYS?
ACT CASUAL! ACT CASUAL!!
Peirce

GOT YOUR EYE ON THAT FIGURINE, SON ?
HUH?... YES!... UM... IT'S... WELL... HOW MUCH DOES IT COST?

CHUCKLE! WELL, HOW MUCH DO YOU HAVE ?
UH... LET ME CHECK.

HOW MUCH DO WE HAVE?

"WE"?
EXCUSE US WHILE WE CONDUCT A BRIEF INVESTORS' MEETING.
Peirce

FRANCIS, GIVE ME TEN DOLLARS!
WHAT? WHY DRAG ME INTO THIS?

BECAUSE THIS IS A SURE THING! WE BUY THIS FIGURINE FOR TEN BUCKS, AND SELL IT FOR A HUNDRED! WE'LL MAKE A HUGE PROFIT! WE'LL BE RICH!

ARE YOU SURE THAT THING IS WORTH A HUNDRED BUCKS?
POSITIVE! TRUST ME!

THAT'S WHAT YOU SAID WHEN YOU CONVINCED ME TO INVEST IN YOUR "FUDGE-ON-A-STICK" BUSINESS.
...WHICH WOULD HAVE WORKED IF NOT FOR THAT HEAT WAVE.
Peirce

SUCCESS! WE NOW OWN A VINTAGE CAPTAIN VOLTAGE FIGURINE! WHAT AN INVESTMENT!
SO NOW WHAT DO WE DO?
YARD SALE
TODAY 10 - 3

WE TAKE IT DOWN TO KLASSIC KOMIX AND SELL IT! FOR A HUNDRED SMACKERS!

THEN WE JUST SIT BACK AND LIVE OFF OUR PROFITS!
F

LIVE OFF $45 EACH?
NO, NO, WE USE THE $45 TO BUY STOCK!
Peirce

HEY, CHUCKLES! WHY THE LONG FACE?
HMMPH.

HMMPH WHAT?
READ THIS QUOTE.

"A CARTOONIST NEEDS TO BE A GOOD ARTIST, NOT A GREAT ARTIST, AND A GOOD WRITER, NOT A GREAT WRITER."

OKAY. SO?
SO... **I** WANT TO BE A CARTOONIST!

...BUT I'M A GREAT ARTIST! **AND** A GREAT WRITER!

I'M OVER-QUALIFIED.

RIGHT.
NOW I'LL HAVE TO SETTLE FOR BEING **PRESIDENT** OR SOME-THING!

GORDIE, MY MAN!
HI, NATE! HERE FOR THE NEW ISSUE OF "FEMME FATALITY"?

NOPE! FRANCIS AND I ARE HERE TO CASH IN!

SEE THIS CAPTAIN VOLTAGE FIGURINE? GUESS HOW MUCH WE PAID FOR IT AT A YARD SALE!

TEN BUCKS?
NOPE! TEN BU–... WAIT, WHAT?
Peirce

...AND IT'S GOT TO BE WORTH AT **LEAST** A HUNDRED DOLLARS!
LET ME GET WAYNE. HE'S AN EXPERT ON COLLECT-IBLES.

WHO'S WAYNE?
THE BOSS.
WAYNE!

MUMBLE MUMBLE MUMBLE MUMBLE MUMBLE MUMBLE

THE BOSS OF **WHAT**?
YIKES.
MUMBLE MUMBLE MUMBLE MUMBLE MUMBLE MUMBLE
Peirce

THAT FIGURINE BETTER BE WORTH WHAT YOU **SAY** IT IS, NATE!
UMBLE
UMBLE
MUMBLE
MUMBLE
MUMBLE

THAT TEN BUCKS WE USED TO **BUY** IT WAS FOR GETTING MY GRANDMA A **BIRTHDAY** GIFT!
YOU CAN **RELAX**, FRANCIS! GRANDMA'S GOING TO GET HER GIFT!

SNORT!
NUH-UH.

HOW WOULD THE OLD GAL FEEL ABOUT AN I.O.U?
peirce

SORRY, GUYS. WAYNE SAYS ONLY **FIRST EDITION** CAPTAIN VOLTAGE FIGURINES ARE WORTH A HUNDRED DOLLARS.

YOURS IS **FOURTH** EDITION. IT'S PRETTY COMMON.
SO... IT'S ONLY WORTH TEN BUCKS?

NO, NO. NOT TEN BUCKS.
AH-HA!

TWO BUCKS.
OH HO...

NICE **JOB**, NATE! YOU SPENT **MY** TEN DOLLARS TO BUY A WORTHLESS PIECE OF **JUNK**!
I KNOW, I KNOW.

YOU OWE ME TEN DOLLARS, NATE! **NOW**!
I DON'T HAVE IT **ON** ME, FRANCIS! **DUH**!

BUT YOU DO **HAVE** IT... RIGHT?
OF **COURSE** I DO! IT'S AT **HOME**!

LATER...
CAN I HAVE TEN BUCKS?
Peirce

NATE, I'M NOT GOING TO JUST **HAND** YOU TEN DOLLARS SO YOU CAN MAKE YOUR MISTAKE MAGICALLY **DISAPPEAR**!

YOU BORROWED MONEY FROM FRANCIS TO BUY THAT THING, SO **YOU** NEED TO EARN THE MONEY TO PAY HIM BACK!
OKAY, OKAY...

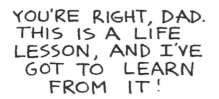

YOU'RE RIGHT, DAD. THIS IS A LIFE LESSON, AND I'VE GOT TO LEARN FROM IT!

LATER...
... AND THAT'S THE **ORIGINAL PAINT**!
WOW!
POTENTIALLY PRICELESS FIGURINE $15
Peirce

SPITSY, IT'S TIME FOR A LITTLE TALK.

YOU'RE AFRAID OF SQUIRRELS, YOU PLAY WITH CATS, YOU WEAR A WUSSY SWEATER AND A COLLAR THAT LOOKS LIKE A SATELLITE DISH...

WAG WAG
WAG WAG

BASICALLY, YOU'RE A DISGRACE TO DOGS EVERYWHERE.
BUT I HAVE A **PLAN**!
WURF!

I'M GOING TO TEACH YOU HOW TO PLAY FRISBEE! THEN AT LEAST YOU'LL HAVE **ONE** SKILL THAT'S "DOGGY"!

READY? HERE WE GO! YOU KNOW WHAT TO DO, RIGHT?

NAB!

ZING!

BONK!
! !
OW!

? ?
GOOD DOG!
Peirce

OKAY, BOYS, IT'S OUR SEASON FINALE! BIG GAME! **BIG** GAME!
CLAP CLAP CLAP

"BIG GAME"? WE'RE NOT EVEN GOING TO MAKE THE **PLAYOFFS**! WHAT'S SO BIG ABOUT THIS GAME?

THE OPPOSING PITCHER.

GRUNT!
SNORT!
I'M GUESSING SIX-TWO, 255.
YIKES.
Peirce

GUYS, SINCE TODAY'S OUR LAST GAME, I DECIDED TO HAVE SOME FUN WITH THE LINEUP!
COACH

I'M GIVING EACH OF YOU THE CHANCE TO PLAY A DIFFERENT POSITION!
OOH! COACH! WHERE AM I PLAYING?

YOU'RE PITCHING, NATE...
I AM? YES!

YES! YES!
...BUT FOR HOW LONG REMAINS TO BE SEEN.
Peirce

COACH, I'VE NEVER PLAYED CATCHER BEFORE. WHAT IF I STINK AT IT?
WHAT IF YOU'RE **GREAT** AT IT?
ACH

JUST DO YOUR BEST, CHAD... AND REMEMBER, YOU'RE NOT ALONE OUT THERE! YOU'VE GOT YOUR **PITCHER** TO HELP YOU!
HELP ME?

CHAD, M'BOY!

HELP ME.
CAN YOU CATCH A SPLIT-FINGER KNUCKLE SLURVE?
PEIRCE

FINALLY I GET THE CHANCE TO PITCH! IT'S ABOUT TIME!

THESE GUYS WILL NEVER KNOW WHAT HIT THEM!

POW

I, ON THE OTHER HAND, DON'T HAVE THAT PROB-LEM.
IT'S STILL RISING!

SO, CHAD... IS MY STUFF NASTY?
WHAT?

YOU KNOW... JOSH BECKETT'S STUFF IS NASTY! ROY HALLADAY'S STUFF IS **NASTY**!
I DON'T KNOW THOSE GUYS.

...BUT YOUR STUFF SURE SEEMS NASTY TO **ME**! **REALLY** NASTY! I MEAN, IT'S **DISGUSTING**!

IT'S **RANCID**! IT'S **PUTRID**! IT'S...
GET BACK BEHIND THE PLATE, CHAD.
PEIRCE

I'M GOING TO MAKE A PITCHING CHANGE, NATE.
WHAT? WHY?

YOU LOOK A LITTLE TIRED.
ME? I'M NOT TIRED! I'M JUST GETTING WARMED UP!

A STARTING PITCHER SHOULD GO THE WHOLE GAME! I'VE ONLY GONE THROUGH THEIR BATTING ORDER TWICE!

...IN THE FIRST INNING.
...BUT WITH A TRIPLE PLAY, I'LL BE OUT OF IT!
COACH

IT'S SEPTEMBER 4TH.
YUP.

VACATION'S ALMOST OVER.
UH-HUH.

TOMORROW'S LABOR DAY.
YES IT IS.

SCHOOL STARTS IN 43½ HOURS.
YOU ARE CORRECT.

THINK WE SHOULD START WORKING ON OUR SUMMER READING LIST?
HEH HEH...

WA HA HA HA
HA HA HA HA
HA HA HA HA

HEH HEH! HA
HA HA HEH
HA HA WHEEEW!
HEH

NO.
RIGHT. THERE'S STILL TIME.
Peirce

RRRING!
NYA!

SCHOOL BELL! SCHOOL BELL!
NATE! NATE!

IT'S MY PHONE, YOU PINHEAD! MY MOM IS CALLING ME!
WHEW!
GASP! GASP!
RRING!

HI.
NOTEBOOK SHOPPING? SURE!
NYA!
Peirce

A 3-day weekend's
Quite a treat
For working men
And women.
ICNIC
AREA

That extra day
Means time to play,
Camp out, or
Have fun swimmin'.

For three full days
Of R & R,
You neither rush
Nor race.

And then the fourth
Day comes along
And smacks you
In the face.
SCHOOL
ZONE
Peirce

WELCOME BACK, BOYS! HAVE YOU HEARD ABOUT OUR NEW SCHOOL MOTTO?

"P.S. 38: WE'RE ALL IN IT TOGETHER"!

LIKE IT? IT'S SORT OF A PLAY ON WORDS!

THAT'S CATCHY!
I'M GETTING A HEADACHE.
Peirce

UH... YEAH, OKAY.

HMPH.

WHAT'S THE MATTER?

WHEN THE DETENTION MONITOR SAYS "SEE YOU THIS AFTERNOON" ON THE FIRST DAY OF SCHOOL, YOU KNOW WHERE YOU STAND.
Peirce

I'M GOING TO TRY TO GET ALONG WITH MRS. GODFREY THIS YEAR! I'LL WIN HER OVER BY BEING SUPER FRIENDLY!

HI, MRS. GODFREY! HA! HA! HOW ARE YOU?

WHY ARE YOU LAUGHING, NATE? ARE YOU TRYING TO BE FUNNY?
WHAT? NO, I... IT WAS A WARM CHUCKLE!

DO I AMUSE YOU?
IT WAS A WARM CHUCKLE!
Peirce

MRS. GODFREY, I HAVE A SEATING CHART QUESTION.

HOW COME YOU MAKE US SIT IN A BOY-GIRL-BOY-GIRL PATTERN?

NATE, SURELY YOU'RE MATURE ENOUGH THAT YOU DON'T OBJECT TO SITTING NEAR GIRLS.
GIRLS? NO.
Peirce

GIRL. SINGULAR.
MRS. GODFREY, CAN I GET EXTRA CREDIT FOR FINISHING THE WORK-SHEET FIRST?

AWW, THIS IS **SWEET**! BUILDING A SAND CASTLE, KIDDIES?
SOMETHING LIKE THAT.

BETTER LOOK **OUT**, SCRUBS! I MIGHT JUST **KNOCK IT OVER**!
NO, YOU WON'T.

YEAH? WELL, I'LL COME BACK LATER AND WE'LL **SEE** ABOUT THAT!
FINE.
9
11

YOU WON'T KNOCK IT OVER.

LATER...

!
Peirce

MR. ROSA, MY GOAL IN ART THIS YEAR IS TO CREATE A **MASTERPIECE!**

AN ENDURING WORK OF CREATIVE GENIUS THAT DEFINES MY ARTISTIC **CAREER!**
WONDER-FUL!

JUST MAKE SURE, WHATEVER IT IS, THAT IT FITS INTO THE CUBBYHOLE I'VE ASSIGNED YOU!

THEY TELL YOU TO THINK OUTSIDE THE BOX, BUT THEY REALLY DON'T WANT YOU TO THINK OUTSIDE THE BOX.
Peirce

WHAT'S ALL THIS?
I TOLD YOU I WAS GOING TO CREATE A MASTER-PIECE!

THESE ARE MY PLANS FOR A HUGE MURAL I'M GOING TO PAINT! THE THEME IS "GREAT FIGURES IN WORLD HISTORY"!

THAT'S A LOT TO FIT IN A MURAL!
I KNOW. I'M HAVING TROUBLE FIGURING OUT WHO'S IN AND WHO'S OUT.

DWAYNE "THE ROCK" JOHNSON MAY END UP ON THE CUTTING ROOM FLOOR.
WELL, THERE'S A FIRST TIME FOR EVERY-THING.
Peirce

PRINCIPAL NICHOLS! CAN I PAINT A MURAL IN THE CAFETORIUM?
WE ALREADY **HAVE** A MURAL, NATE.

BUT THAT'S JUST A PAINTING OF TREES AND FLOWERS! **MINE** WOULD SHOW GREAT FIGURES IN WORLD HISTORY!

HM! YOU'VE GOT QUITE A LINEUP HERE!
YES, I DO!

NOW, WHO IS...?
THAT'S ME. RIGHT NEXT TO ZACH GALIFIANAKIS.
PEIRCE

NATE, I SPOKE TO THE SCHOOL IMPROVEMENT COMMITTEE ABOUT YOUR MURAL PROPOSAL.
YES! SO CAN I GET STARTED?

NOT JUST YET. FIRST THE COMMITTEE WILL RECOMMEND SEVERAL CHANGES TO THE LIST OF HISTORICAL FIGURES DEPICTED.

...AND INSTEAD OF ALLOWING YOU TO PAINT IT ALL BY YOUR**SELF**, WE'RE GOING TO INVOLVE **ALL** THE STUDENTS!

...BUT OTHER THAN **THAT**, THEY **LOVE** THE IDEA!
OH, AND IT WON'T EXACTLY BE A MURAL!
Peirce

YOU LOOK UPSET, NATE.
PRINCIPAL NICHOLS TOTALLY RUINED MY IDEA!

MY PLAN WAS: I PAINT A GIANT MURAL IN THE CAFETORIUM THAT WILL LAST FOR YEARS!... DECADES!... FOREVER!

HIS PLAN IS: ALL THE KIDS IN THE SCHOOL MAKE INDIVIDUAL PAINTINGS ON PIECES OF POSTER-BOARD!

POSTERBOARD ISN'T FOREVER.
THIS IS BARELY A STEP UP FROM PIPE-CLEANER SCULPTURE.
Peirce

GREAT. INSTEAD OF PAINTING A MURAL OF HISTORICAL FIGURES THAT I CHOSE...

...I'M PAINTING AN 18" × 24" POSTER OF SOME GUY THAT THE SCHOOL IMPROVEMENT COMMITTEE CHOSE!

ARRG!
SPLAT
SPLOT
SPLURCH
SPLICH

CALVIN COOLIDGE DIDN'T HAVE AN AFRO.
IT'S A SILENT PROTEST.
Peirce

A BALL CAN'T ACCELERATE ALL BY ITSELF! ACCORDING TO THE LAWS OF PHYSICS, IT STARTS TO DECELERATE AS SOON AS IT'S KICKED!

OOH! CAN I LOOK AT THE PAPER, DAD? I HAVE TO READ MY HOROSCOPE!

THIS WILL TELL ME HOW I'M GOING TO PLAY IN OUR SOCCER GAME TODAY!

HOROSCOPES ARE SUCH A CROCK.
PEIRCE

READY FOR THE BIG GAME?
I'M NOT SURE. MY HOROSCOPE STINKS TODAY.

OH, COME ON! HOROSCOPES DON'T MEAN ANYTHING!
THEY DO FOR ME, TEDDY! I'M A SCORPIO!

THE LIVES OF SCORPIOS ARE GOVERNED BY THE STARS MORE THAN ANY OTHER SIGN!

PLUS, WE'RE CHOCK-FULL OF ANIMAL MAGNETISM!
ROWR!
...WHICH ALWAYS COMES IN HANDY DURING A MIDDLE-SCHOOL SOCCER GAME.
PEIRCE

I'M GOING TO COUNTERACT MY BAD HOROSCOPE WITH A BUNCH OF GOOD LUCK CHARMS! MAYBE THEN WE'LL WIN OUR GAME!

BIG GAME TODAY, BOYS! ARE YOU READY?
YUP!

I'VE GOT MY LUCKY SOCKS, MY LUCKY CLEATS, MY LUCKY KNEE PADS, MY LUCKY GLOVES...

... MY LUCKY RABBIT'S FOOT, MY LUCKY... WAIT... IT'S NOT HERE! WHERE IS IT?...

WHERE'S MY LUCKY "SPONGEBOB" WRIST BAND??
HE'S NOT READY.
Peirce

NATE, YOU'RE A GOOD GOALKEEPER. DO YOU REALLY NEED TO RELY ON SO MANY GOOD LUCK CHARMS?
ACH

WHAT WOULD HAPPEN IF YOU JUST WENT OUT THERE AND **PLAYED**, WITHOUT ALL THE SUPER-STITIONS?
HMM. I'M NOT SURE.

LET ME ASK MY MAGIC 8-BALL.
SHAKE SHAKE SHAKE SHAKE

"YOU DON'T WANT TO KNOW." WELL, **THAT'S** NOT GOOD.
ACH
Peirce

MAYBE COACH IS RIGHT. MAYBE MY LOUSY HOROSCOPE **WON'T** AFFECT HOW I PLAY!

AFTER ALL, WHAT DO **STARS AND PLANETS** HAVE TO DO WITH **SOCCER**?

WHAM!

Peirce

VIVACIOUS? NO. VIGOROUS? NO.

WELL! **SOME**ONE'S WORKING HARD! SCHOOL PROJECT?
YUP.

FOR WHICH CLASS?
CLASS?

HMMMMMM...

TOUGH QUESTION, APPARENTLY.
IT'S PART MATH, PART "WALTER SCOTT'S PERSONALITY PARADE"!
Peirce

IT'S **SORT** OF A SCHOOL PROJECT! I'M TAB-ULATING THE **Q** SCORES OF EVERYONE AT P.S. 38!
Q SCORES?

IT'S AN APPROVAL RATING SYSTEM! IF EVERYBODY KNOWS YOU AND LIKES YOU, YOUR Q SCORE IS ONE HUNDRED!

AND IF NOBODY LIKES YOU, YOUR Q SCORE IS ZERO?
IN MOST CASES.

FOR MRS. GODFREY, I FEEL IT'S MY DUTY TO EXPAND INTO NEGATIVE NUMBERS.
THAT'S VERY RESPONSIBLE OF YOU.
Peirce

YOU GUYS WANNA HEAR YOUR Q SCORES?
WHAT?
SURE!

TEDDY, YOU'RE A 96. FRANCIS, YOU'RE A 93.
HOLD IT, HOLD IT! HOW COME TEDDY'S SCORE IS HIGHER THAN MINE?

BECAUSE TEDDY CAN TAKE A JOKE.
WHAT, AND I CAN'T? I CAN DEFINITELY TAKE A JOKE! I LOVE JOKES!

OOP. YOU'RE DOWN TO AN 89.
I AM NOT!
Peirce

WHAT'S THIS NONSENSE ABOUT A LIST OF PEOPLE'S Q SCORES?
IT'S NOT NONSENSE, GINA! GOT IT RIGHT HERE!

...AND, MIGHT I ADD, YOUR SCORE IS NOTHING TO WRITE HOME ABOUT!
WHAT? WHO SAYS? YOU'RE MAKING THAT UP!

NO, I'M NOT! I'VE SURVEYED PEOPLE! PEOPLE WITH OPINIONS!
WHO? WHO HAVE YOU TALKED TO?

THAT'S HIGHLY CONFIDENTIAL.
YOU'RE MAKING IT UP!!

PRINCIPAL NICHOLS, WOULD YOU LIKE TO EXAMINE THE Q SCORES OF ALL THE TEACHERS? IT'S **VERY** INTERESTING!

AS YOU CAN SEE, **MRS. GODFREY'S** Q SCORE IS THE LOWEST! NOBODY CAN **STAND** THIS WOMAN! SHE'S AN EMBARRASSMENT TO THE SCHOOL!

THIS INFORMATION COULD COME IN HANDY THE NEXT TIME YOU'RE DOING HIRINGS AND... AHEM!... **FIRINGS,** IF YOU GET MY DRIFT!
WINKA WINKA WINKA

YOU'RE AN UNUSUAL BOY.
NO NEED TO THANK ME, BIG FELLA! I'M HERE TO **SERVE!**
Peirce

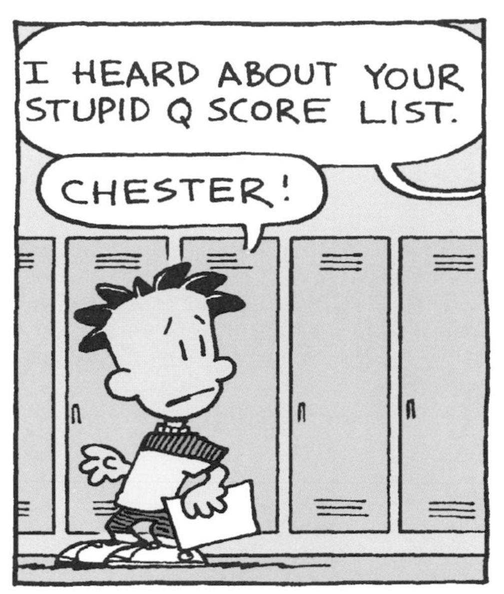
I HEARD ABOUT YOUR STUPID Q SCORE LIST.
CHESTER!

LEMME SEE IT.
BUT... IT... UH... YOU... ULP!

IT... IT'S A REVERSE LIST! THE PEOPLE WITH LOW SCORES ARE ACTUALLY THE MOST POPULAR!! HEH HEH! HA... HA...

THAT BIN IS ONLY FOR RECYCLABLES.
SORRY.
Peirce

RACE YOU TO THE MAILBOX, FRANCIS!
NAH.

WHY **NOT**?
I DON'T WANT TO, THAT'S ALL.

I'M NOT AS COMPETITIVE AS YOU ARE, NATE. I DON'T TURN EVERYTHING INTO A CONTEST.

I'M NOT OBSESSED WITH WHO'S THE FASTEST OR THE STRONGEST OR THE MOST TALENTED.

YOU'RE JUST AFRAID I'LL **BEAT** YOU!
NO, I'M NOT.

WHAT IF I GIVE YOU A HEAD START?
NO.
HOW 'BOUT WE PLAY A GAME OF "HORSE"?
NUH-UH.

LET'S **ARM WRESTLE**, THEN!
NOPE.

YAH!
I'M WINNING!
Peirce

SCHOOL PICTURE GUY!
IN THE FLESH, KID! IN THE FLESH!
SMILE

I HAVE A FREE PERIOD. CAN I HANG OUT WITH YOU?
A TOP-NOTCH IDEA, CHUM! I COULD USE THE HELP!

I'VE GOT A CLASS OF FIRST-GRADERS UP NEXT, AND THEY CAN BE A BIT OF A HANDFUL!

I THINK I'M ABOUT TO THROW UP.
OKAY, CHAMP, SHOW TIME.
Peirce

OKAY, KID, HERE'S THE DRILL: I TAKE THE GLAMOUR SHOTS, YOU WRANGLE THE CATTLE.
HUH?
SMILE

GET THE CHILDREN UP ON THE STOOL, AND TRY TO MAKE 'EM SMILE!
GOTCHA!
SMILE

OKAY, MIRANDA, YOU'RE UP!
NO.

NO! NO! NO!
WELCOME TO MY WORLD, AMIGO.
SMILE
Peirce

OKAY, JIMMY, THAT'S A GOOD SMILE, BUT YOU NEED TO OPEN YOUR EYES.

WHOOP. NOT **THAT** MUCH. YOU LOOK LIKE YOU JUST DRANK A GALLON OF "RED BULL."

...AND **NOW** YOU LOOK LIKE YOU'RE EITHER ABOUT TO PASS OUT, OR...

SNIF!
WAAH!
OKAY, LET'S START OVER.
Peirce

NICE JOB, MASON. YOU'RE ALL DONE.
DO I GET A LOLLI-POP?

UH... I DON'T THINK...
AT MY OLD SCHOOL, I GOT A LOLLIPOP AFTER MY PICTURE!
SNIF!

OKAY... WELL... UH... LOOK! I'VE GOT A SOURBALL YOU CAN HAVE!...
OOH! YUMMY!

WE WANT SOUR-BALLS TOO!
BAD MOVE, KID.
Peirce

NO OFFENSE, SCHOOL PICTURE GUY, BUT A LOT OF THE SHOTS FROM THAT LAST SESSION AREN'T SO GREAT.
UH-HUH.

MOST OF THESE KIDS AREN'T EVEN SMILING.
RIGHT.

...AND HALF OF 'EM HAVE THEIR EYES CLOSED!
EXACTLY.
SMILE

YOU'RE TAKING LOUSY PICTURES ON PURPOSE!
SSSH!
SMILE
Peirce

LET'S GET SOMETHING STRAIGHT, KID: I DON'T **TRY** TO MAKE PEOPLE LOOK BAD IN THEIR SCHOOL PICTURES...
SMILE

...BUT SOMETIMES IT JUST **HAPPENS!** EYELIDS DROOP! NOSES RUN! THAT'S LIFE!

THEN THEIR PARENTS BRING 'EM BACK ON RE-SHOOT DAY AND PAY ME FOR **MORE** PICTURES!
SMILE

AND THOSE ARE BETTER?
NO, THEY'RE WORSE. IT'S **HILARIOUS!**
SMILE
Peirce

...AND WHAT WAS THE NAME OF HAMILTON'S OPPONENT?...
...NATE.
ME?

UMMM...
OOH!

WHAT'S YOUR PROBLEM, GINA?
I'M RAISING MY HAND!

EXCUSE ME, BUT I'M ANSWERING THE QUESTION!
SNORT! RIGHT. LIKE YOU KNOW THE ANSWER!

OH, YEAH? WHAT MAKES YOU SO SURE I DON'T?
TAP TAP

I HAPPEN TO BE THINKING OF THE ANSWER THIS VERY MINUTE!
YAWNNNN...

...AND THE ANSWER IIIIIIIS...
...I.M. GASSY!

HA HA HA HA HA HA
HA HA HA HA HA
YOU'RE A RIOT.
HA HA HA HA HA
Peirce

I WONDER HOW MUCH LONGER JENNY AND ARTUR WILL LAST AS A COUPLE.
HOLD IT, HOLD IT.

I THOUGHT YOU WERE **OVER** JENNY!
I **AM** OVER HER, FRANCIS! COM**PLETE**LY!

I'M JUST ASKING, AS A DISINTERESTED THIRD PARTY WITH NO AGENDA WHATSOEVER...

...WHEN SHE'S GOING TO **DUMP** THIS LOSER!
HOW NICE TO KNOW YOU'VE MOVED ON.
Peirce

I THINK JENNY IS TOO YOUNG TO HAVE A STEADY BOYFRIEND.
SNORT! UNLESS **YOU** WERE HER BOY-FRIEND! **THEN** SHE WOULDN'T BE TOO YOUNG!

WHY WOULD IT BE OKAY FOR JENNY TO DATE **YOU**, BUT IT'S **NOT** OKAY FOR HER TO DATE **ARTUR**?

BECAUSE I'M ME.

RIGHT. I FORGOT.
WELL, COME **ON**, FRANCIS! **THINK!**
Peirce

IT JUST DOESN'T ADD UP.
WHAT DOESN'T?

WHY JENNY PREFERS **ARTUR** TO **ME**! HERE'S THE ARTUR COLUMN, AND HERE'S THE NATE COLUMN!

HE'S GOOD AT MATH, SCIENCE AND MAKING THE HONOR ROLL. **I'M** GOOD AT SPORTS, CARTOONING, AND BEING SMOLDERINGLY CHARISMATIC.

ADVANTAGE, MOI.
BY A LAND-SLIDE.
PEIRCE

I THINK I KNOW WHY JENNY LIKES ARTUR BETTER THAN ME!
DO TELL.

IT'S THE GOOFY WAY HE TALKS! FOR SOME REASON, EVERYBODY THINKS HIS FRACTURED ENGLISH IS CHARMING!

SO ALL I HAVE TO DO TO WIN JENNY'S HEART IS START TALKING IN STUPID-SOUNDING GIBBERISH!

"START"?
WHEN DOES THE CHARMING PART KICK IN?
Peirce

STILL TRYING TO BREAK UP JENNY AND ARTUR?
I'M **NOT** TRYING TO BREAK THEM UP, FRANCIS!

I'M JUST SHOWING JENNY THAT I HAVE A LOT TO OFFER!... THAT I'M PRIME BOYFRIEND MATERIAL!

MAYBE SHE'LL READ THIS AND REALIZE THAT I'M HER **SOUL MATE**!

FYI, "ARTUR" AND "MANURE" DON'T REALLY RHYME.
EXCUSE ME, IT'S **FREE VERSE**!
Peirce

ALL RIGHT, JENNY, I'M GOING TO LAY MY CARDS ON THE TABLE.

I'VE KNOWN YOU A LONG TIME, SO I'M UNIQUELY QUALIFIED TO SAY THAT YOUR CURRENT BOYFRIEND JUST ISN'T **RIGHT** FOR YOU!

YOU CAN DO BETTER, JENNY. YOU CAN DO **WAY** BETTER.

NO OFFENSE, ARTUR.
BUT WAIT. I THOUGHT YOU SAY WE ARE TO PLAYING **CARDS**.
Peirce

OKAY, I'VE GOT EVERYTHING I NEED! THANKS, ARTUR!
WHAT WAS **THAT** ABOUT?
I'M GOING TO PROVE ONCE AND FOR ALL THAT ARTUR AND JENNY **AREN'T** A PERFECT COUPLE!

I JUST ASKED ARTUR TWENTY QUESTIONS ABOUT HIMSELF! NOW I'LL ASK JENNY THE EXACT SAME QUESTIONS!

...AND I BET HER ANSWERS WILL SHOW THAT THE TWO OF THEM HAVE **NOTHING** IN COMMON!

THEIR RELATIONSHIP WILL **CRUMBLE!**
OOH! JENNY! I HAVE SOME QUESTIONS FOR YOU!

FIRST QUESTION: *AHEM!* WHAT'S YOUR FAVORITE PASTIME?

HERE HE COMES NOW!

ANY QUESTIONS?
FOR WHAT IT'S WORTH, **HIS** ANSWER WAS "STAMP COLLECTING."
Peirce

...AND WHEN DID THAT BILL BECOME LAW?
OOH!

DO YOU **HAVE** TO DO THAT, GINA? YOU SOUND LIKE YOU'RE IN THE MIDDLE OF A **TENNIS MATCH**!

YOU'RE LIKE ONE OF THOSE PLAYERS WHO SCREAMS EVERY TIME THEY HIT THE BALL!

IS THERE A **PROBLEM**, NATE?
...AND HERE COMES THE CHAIR UMPIRE.

I'M GOING TO BEAT GINA TO THE PUNCH ON THIS NEXT QUESTION! THEN SHE'LL SEE HOW **ANNOYING** IT IS!

WHAT WAS THE FIRST BATTLE OF THE...
OOH!

YOU INTERRUPTED ME, NATE. THAT'S VERY RUDE.

DETENTION.
OH, HOW I HATE HER.

LOOK, MRS. GODFREY! "NO LOUD VOICES"! IT'S ONE OF YOUR CLASSROOM RULES!
NO LOUD VOICES

SO HOW COME YOU LET GINA SCREAM "OOH" AT THE TOP OF HER LUNGS WHENEVER SHE RAISES HER HAND?

BECAUSE, NATE, WHEN A STUDENT FEELS PASSIONATELY ABOUT SOMETHING, IT'S MY JOB TO BE ENCOURAGING, NOT DISCOURAGING.

NOW SIT DOWN AND PUT YOUR HEAD ON YOUR DESK.
GREAT
Peirce

IT'S SO **OBVIOUS** THAT **GINA** IS MRS. GODFREY'S **FAVORITE**! I THOUGHT TEACHERS WERE SUPPOSED TO TREAT EVERYONE THE **SAME**!

WELL, IF YOU OWNED TWO CATS, AND ONE OF THEM WAS WELL-BEHAVED AND THE OTHER WAS ALWAYS SCRATCHING THE FURNITURE, WHICH WOULD **YOU** PREFER?

KNOW WHAT I MEAN?

I WOULD **NEVER** OWN A CAT.
HE DOESN'T KNOW WHAT I MEAN.
PEIRCE

MR. ROSA, TEACHERS AREN'T SUPPOSED TO PLAY FAVORITES, RIGHT?

WELL, **MRS. GODFREY** DOES! **GINA'S** HER FAVORITE! IT'S SO **ANNOYING!**

NATE, YOU KNOW I CAN'T DISCUSS MRS. GODFREY WITH YOU.
YEAH...

SO LET'S DISCUSS **GINA**, THEN! SHE IS SUCH A...
STOP.
Peirce

YOU'RE RIGHT, NATE. TEACHERS AREN'T SUPPOSED TO HAVE FAVORITE STUDENTS.
BUT?...

BUT WHAT?
BUT THEY **DO**! ALL TEACHERS HAVE FAVORITES DEEP DOWN! IT'S SO **OBVIOUS**!

I MEAN, IT'S COMMON KNOWLEDGE THAT I'M **YOUR** PERSONAL FAVORITE!

IT IS?
YEAH, BUT I DON'T FLAUNT IT. I KEEP IT ON THE DOWN-LOW.
Peirce

WHAT'S TAKING HIM SO LONG?
HE SAYS HE'LL ONLY BUY A PUMPKIN THAT SPEAKS TO HIM.
KINS
9¢ LB.

...THAT **SPEAKS** TO HIM?
RIGHT.

THAT'S WEIRD.
OOP. LOOK.

I THINK HE FOUND ONE.

SO I GUESS THAT ONE SPOKE TO HIM.
GUESS SO.

I WONDER WHAT IT SAID.

SNAP!
THONK!

"DON'T PICK ME UP BY MY STEM."
HE NEVER LISTENS!
Peirce

DAD, CAN I GO TRICK-OR-TREATING IN TEDDY'S NEIGHBORHOOD THIS YEAR?
WHAT'S WRONG WITH **OUR** NEIGHBORHOOD?

IT'S **BORING**! EVERYBODY HANDS OUT THE SAME STUFF!
I DON'T!

I ALWAYS TRY TO PROVIDE A TREAT THAT'S... THAT'S...

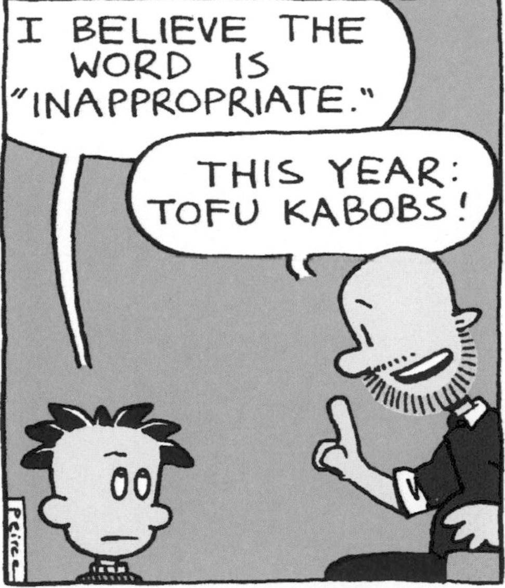
I BELIEVE THE WORD IS "INAPPROPRIATE."
THIS YEAR: TOFU KABOBS!
Peirce

DAD, NO! YOU CAN'T HAND OUT TOFU KABOBS AS A HALLOWEEN TREAT!
YOU'RE RIGHT! WHAT WAS I THINKING?

I HANDED OUT TOFU LAST YEAR! I DON'T WANT TO REPEAT MYSELF!

...OR WAS IT LAST YEAR? HM... I'M NOT SURE... IT MIGHT HAVE BEEN TWO YEARS AGO...

FRANKLY, THE YEARS ARE ALL STARTING TO BLEND TOGETHER.
GOT IT! LAST YEAR WAS FRUIT ROLL-UPS!
SNAP!
Peirce

I DECIDED THAT HANDING OUT TOFU KABOBS FOR HALLOWEEN **WAS** A LITTLE GOOFY!
REALLY?
! !

YUP! INSTEAD, I'M MAKING MY OWN RICE KRISPIE TREATS!
DAD! NICE JOB!

I WAS A BIT CONCERNED ABOUT THE HIGH SUGAR CONTENT, THOUGH, SO I TWEAKED THE RECIPE SLIGHTLY!
CHOMPF!

HNK!
URK!
GGK!
TOO MUCH BARLEY?
Peirce

HOWDY, BOYS!
WHERE'VE YOU **BEEN**? WE ALMOST STARTED WITHOUT YOU!

SORRY. MY DAD MADE RICE KRISPIE TREATS TO HAND OUT, AND I HAD TO HELP HIM PUT THEM IN LITTLE BAGGIES.

...WHICH REMINDS ME, HE SENT THESE ALONG FOR YOU GUYS.
5

THEY... UH... LOOK A LITTLE WEIRD.
WE WERE OUT OF RICE KRISPIES, SO HE USED ACTUAL RICE.
5
Peirce

HEY! I KNOW YOU!

OF COURSE YOU DO! I'M A LAWN GNOME!
NO, I MEAN... I KNOW YOU!

LOOK! IT'S THE KID WHOSE DAD HANDS OUT THOSE STUPID HALLOWEEN TREATS!
HA
HA
HA
HA

HA HA HA HA HA HA
DUDE! YOU'RE FAMOUS!
WHAT IS IT THIS YEAR? CELERY?
Peirce

TRICK OR...
I'M SORRY, BOYS...

I RAN OUT OF CANDY, SO ALL I HAVE LEFT ARE SOME APPLES AND TANGERINES!

THAT'S OKAY, MISTER. NO PROBLEM.
REALLY? SO YOU'RE NOT GOING TO EGG MY HOUSE?

DUDE, YOU'RE TALKING TO A KID WHOSE DAD ONCE HANDED OUT ZESTY RANCH SOY NUTS.
WOW. THAT'S LAME.
Peirce

MOMMY, LOOK AT THE SMURF!

SMURF? THAT KID CALLED ME A SMURF! EXCUSE ME, I'M A LAWN GNOME!

SMURFS AND LAWN GNOMES DON'T LOOK ALIKE! NOT EVEN CLOSE!

SMURFS ARE BLUE! DO I LOOK BLUE TO YOU? NO!

SMURF! *SNORT!* PLEASE!

OOH! ARE YOU A SMURF, LIKE ME?
! !

WHY, YES I AM!
QUICK COSTUME CHANGE.
Peirce

Big Nate is distributed internationally by Universal Uclick.

Andrews McMeel Publishing, LLC
an Andrews McMeel Universal company
1130 Walnut Street, Kansas City, Missouri 64106

www.andrewsmcmeel.com

15 16 17 18 19 SDB 10 9 8 7 6 5 4 3 2 1

ISBN: 978-1-4494-6226-0

Library of Congress Control Number: 2015937249

Made by:
Shenzhen Donnelley Printing Company Ltd.
Address and location of manufacturer:
No. 47, Wuhe Nan Road, Bantian Ind. Zone,
Shenzhen China, 518129
1st Printing—6/22/15

These strips appeared in newspapers from
May 15, 2011, through October 30, 2011.

Big Nate can be viewed on the Internet at
www.gocomics.com/big_nate